THE HIGHER GENIUS

Magical Tales of New York City

THE HIGHER GENIUS

Magical Tales of New York City

Kyler James

REBEL SATORI PRESS

New Orleans & New York

Published in the United States of America by
Rebel Satori Press
www.rebelsatoripress.com

Cover art: Andrew Ostrovsky
Book design: Sven Davisson

Title font: Castine™ 1998 by Brian Willson/Three Islands Press (3IP)

Paperback ISBN: 978-1-60864-282-3
Ebook ISBN: 978-1-60864-283-0

for Angel
for encouraging me to do this book.

Contents

PART ONE:
NONFICTION

THE MAD SCIENTIST

The only duty and destiny we acknowledged
was that each one of us should become so completely
himself, so utterly faithful to the active seed which
Nature planted within him, that in living out its
growth he could be surprised by nothing unknown to
come.

– Hermann Hesse, *Demian*

When I was very young, my parents took me to a psychologist. They
told me he was an allergist, but I didn't believe them. He asked me what
my three wishes were – and I'll never forget my Big Three:

1. to have a magic wand,
2. to be the only person in the world with a magic wand – and,
3. to never have my magic wand taken away.

Well now as an adult, my first wish at least has come true: I have
my magic wand. It represents the magical will, the element of fire, the
phallus. I call it simply, my wand. It's carved out of wood with a big
quartz crystal at the tip, wrapped in copper wire. It's consecrated and
charged with power: it has helped me to become who I am.

One night my wand proved to me just how powerful it was. I

happened to be playing strip-poker – and I was losing miserably. I was in a desperate state and needed to do something fast. So like the three fairies in Disney's *Sleeping Beauty* who retrieved their hidden wands, I decided to use magic and fetch mine.

From that moment on, literally, I got hand after hand of full-houses, straights, flushes and royal flushes. I was saved from humiliation in strip-poker! My wand, I realized, was endowed with the magical power I had given it. Coincidence, you say? Good point: for everything in magic *seems* like coincidence, but it's the frequency and timeliness of these "coincidences" that could knock the hardest-nosed skeptic off his rocker!

I've got five magical tools altogether, wand included, each with its own function, each representing an element of nature. This may all sound amusingly crazy – and yes, I *am* crazy, but I am oh, so brilliantly sane! With my magical tools, I have created myself: Kyler, the psychic – Kyler, the magician. And with the tools of magic you can create yourself too.

See, I've always been smart – a straight-A student all through school. I've applied my intelligence to the study of magic and integrated everything I've ever learned to the realization of magical truth in my life. Through this process, I am able to assist many people with valuable information, the fruits of which come from years of hard work, discipline, and frivolity!

I have witnessed miracles; I have created miracles. They are real and true. The fools are the non-believers. Or, the fools are the believers. Which is worse? Which is which? I'm interested in the *doers*, the creators, the Supermen and Superwomen of the world! Let's be heroic, all of us! Let's not succumb to ordinary existence; life is too extraordinary for that.

Who are you, really? Who do you deeply, deeply wish to be?

I'll tell you who I am: I am a mad scientist who lives in his laboratory, a temple of his own imagination. I have shed tears and I have shed blood. At the age of 46 I am here to claim my life. I am my own God. I use my own words. I think my own thoughts. For inside my mind I can ascertain the truth. Inside my mind I can reach you all. And above my mind I can hear the voice of my higher self, my Higher Genius, who gives names and messages with amazing accuracy.

How do I explain myself? Simply this: *I've fought all my life to be me.* Through years of searching, through grieving loneliness – listening to no one save Zarathustra – I have been born unto myself.

So let's explore the magical approach to who we really are. Let's conjure the Magic Circle, the island called Neverland, the land of Eternal Youth. And perhaps you will believe me, for like Peter Pan, "I never lie." It's only the liars who don't believe me.

ADVENTURES ON THE MAGICAL PATH

Sometimes there's God so quickly!

– Tennessee Williams, *A Streetcar Named Desire*

What a magical neighborhood I grew up in! There was magic everywhere – but don't all children create magic out of their surroundings? The fireflies at dusk were secretly fairies; the nuns in white were secretly ghosts; and the woods behind us were definitely enchanted. And all the while the large Star of David from the temple down the street shined on our houses as if to say, "There is power here – there is something bigger than who you are – and you can reach it if you come to me."

My best friend Hank and I ruled the world – or at least our block. I created – and enforced – all of our games. We wore signs on our chests proclaiming who we were: Hank was "Nature". . . and I was "God." (The Goddess and God of my future years.) Together we reigned over Clarendon Court, or at least *I* did, always under the glorified presence of the Star of David, what I now call the Six-Rayed Star.

"Mix-up" was my favorite game. One of us would blindfold the other, spin him around and lead him to familiar parts of our yards. We'd be quizzed on where we actually were. And it was the most astounding feeling to remove the blindfold and to realize that we were standing on our own front steps. Such alternative perceptions of reality, like

Steppenwolf's Magic Theatre! Not until my adult initiations did I experience such a thrill, where the mystery of one world merges into the mystery of the next.

Hank and his brother were eventually forbidden to play with me. Their father wanted his boys to play "normal" games like "Cowboys and Indians" and "Cops and Robbers." Guns were required, not imaginations. And they grew up to be normal, healthy Americans – a lawyer and doctor, respectively. (And respectably.) I was Peter Pan and would never grow up. So I retreated into my fantasy world and gradually became. . . religious!

My father promised my sister and me that if we didn't like Sunday School we wouldn't have to go back after the first day. What a fib, Dad! We were *chained* to Sunday School – and later Hebrew School, which I hated then, but am so grateful for now.

The first time they told us the story of Moses, I was awe inspired. I could think of nothing else all day. What they *didn't* tell us was that Moses was a master magician, trained in Egypt. All the miracles in the Bible were performed by magicians – true magicians as opposed to illusionists. And it was so much easier to wield magic in the days before technology, the days when everyone believed in it, as children do now.

That night I prayed at my bedroom window. I remember the stars in the western sky as I asked God to *please* not send any burning bushes until I was ready. For I knew that one day I *would* be ready, ready for something as high as those stars, as great as our shining Six-Rayed Star, as golden as that day of the Sun, that Sunday, when I first learned about Moses and knew that I too was destined to hear from God.

Thirty years later I'm in my Magic Temple. It's the night and hour of Venus: Friday night, 9:22 PM. (I've calculated this precisely according to the sunset and sunrise from *The New York Times*.) I have cast the

Magic Circle and I am one with The Eternal. With my staff, I call forth one of the Great and Powerful names of God – the same name that Charlton Heston uses in *The Ten Commandments,* only in Hebrew. I'm invoking this special name seven times (the Kabbalistic number of Venus) and suddenly my caldron of incense bursts into flames!

At first I am terrified: this has never happened before. What if my apartment burns down at the hands of a crazy magician? But as the flames continue to flare, I realize I am in the presence of that which I have invoked – and I begin to trust it, knowing I have achieved a new height.

That was a significant night on my Magical Path. The flaming caldron has reoccurred only once since, while invoking the Goddess of the Full Moon, also at the exact moments of invocation. These were important guideposts for me in our skeptical world of technology that wants us all to be mechanized, that insists magic cannot exist, that venerates *organized* religion, yet denigrates as "crazy" any private contact with what these religions call "God."

In this book it will be my long-awaited pleasure to unveil some of the mysteries of magic for you, so that you too can become aware of its power and, if you so desire, incorporate it into your life. Like the Rainbow Bridge from Wagner's *Ring,* let this book be the bridge that links you to Valhalla, the castle of the Gods. For I have ventured there myself and have witnessed its euphoria.

Now: to some of the nitty-gritties of magic. Let's get real. Does magic really work? Does it really exist? I assure you it does – but it takes more than snapping your fingers; it's no panacea for pain or misery. It takes a lot of hard work and discipline, discipline: study, practice and intelligence.

Magic is the greatest thing I know. I'm so lucky to be able to tell you about it. I can't think of a subject that's more misconstrued, more confused with superstition, more divinely idiotic and insane and wonderful. Because it has to do with the power of the Human Mind. It's *all* the mind. As Hesse said, "We create gods and struggle with them... and they bless us." The power of magic – or of the gods – is in each one of us to utilize fully.

Aleister Crowley, the magical genius of the twentieth century, has given the best definition of magic (he spelled it "magick" to differentiate the real thing from magic tricks): "The Science and Art of causing Change to occur in conformity with Will." Simple, right? It's your will to change your hair color, so you dye it bright red – that's magic, or a form of magic.

It was first explained to me this way: magic is like a hammer – you can use it to build a house or to clobber someone over the head – it's still the same hammer; the principles are the same. Strictly speaking, therefore, there are no subdivisions. But for the purpose of our exploration, let us first divide so that later we can be fruitful and multiply.

WHITE MAGIC. This is magic in its simplest essence. It's nearly the equivalent of prayer and meditation. Candles, incense, chanting and trance, rituals in their most heartfelt enactment, the exaltation of one's purest ideals, this form of magic is the most accessible, the easiest to do and the least dangerous. Gods and Goddesses are contacted and glorified. The "change" that occurs "in conformity with Will" is the *self-transformation* that comes from the joy and beauty of the rituals.

BLACK MAGIC. Doesn't the phrase have an alluring ring to it? Watch out. Maleficent was always my favorite Disney witch, but this was one hell of an unhappy lady! "For the first time in sixteen years I shall sleep well tonight," she intones. Really...doesn't she have anything better to do with her time? Very simply, Black Magic has the intention of *harming, avenging, or manipulating* someone against their will, including love spells directed at a specific person. Stay away from it or you'll regret it.

GREY MAGIC. Now we get to an area that's a little more complex. Depending on how you define it, Grey Magic is actually doing "good" for yourself or others: healings, success spells, love spells, as long as they're for general love; but the tricky part is that Grey Magic can turn into either White or Black. It's a very good idea to do a divination first, like Tarot or *I Ching*, to determine which way the magic will go. For instance, a money spell for yourself is fine if it naturally increases your abundance through your own work; but if your aunt dies the next day and leaves you $10,000, you have probably harmed your aunt and will have to pay a big price for that. So proceed, but proceed with caution – and make sure you know what you're doing.

MUNDANE MAGIC. This is the kind of magic that we all do, simply the doing of work or tasks on the earth-plane. But let's not underestimate its importance. For me, the magic of writing this chapter was first to take a train out-of-town, then to find an article about writing by Joyce Carol Oates on my train seat; then in the throes of inspiration, to begin writing furiously and nearly miss my stop; then confined to my hotel room during a thunderstorm, to finish the first section; and finally to type it, correct it and computerize it. Now *that's* magic.

LOW MAGIC. There is no value judgement here; "low" refers to the lowlands, the countryside, where the pagans, witches and country folk did magic. Mostly uneducated, these people used the herbs and ingredients that were available; and incorporating aspects of White and

Grey Magic, performed the rites that were natural and spontaneous to their feelings. The eight great festivals of the year, or Witch's Sabbats, were celebrated with magnificent beauty and merriment. Today, those of us who are magically inclined still honor the sacred "Wheel of the Year," and praise its particular gods, who are really parts of ourselves.

HIGH MAGIC. You'll notice I saved this one for last. That's because High Magic is my central focus here. It's called "high," not because it gives you such a palpable high, but because it was practiced by the educated magicians, wizards, Kabbalists and alchemists in the high, walled cities. Also called the Great Work, the basic goal of High Magic is to exalt oneself to one's highest height, whether you call that God, Goddess, Higher Self, Higher Genius or Holy Guardian Angel. To put it simply, it's the way of striving for – and possibly attaining – genius. There's certainly value in knowing success with the lower forms of magic; but it's the uplift of the spirit, the higher magic, that's the launching of the soul to its star.

This book will not teach you how to do magic; that's not my mission. Perhaps it will inspire you to pursue it on your own if you're interested. But I hope that the *ideas* of magic, especially High Magic, will encourage you to find your True Will, your purpose in life, your greatest self-vision.

Let's talk a little about how I began all this kooky stuff. You might like to know – for a lot of people ask me – and then you can see for yourself if you want to pursue the Magical Path.

When I first visited the magical shops in New York City, the intoxicating bouquet of the incense and oils drove me wild. I had smelled these smells somewhere before. I was so attracted to them that I thought I'd better get away fast, otherwise I might get involved in something really ridiculous. (I had gone through a dangerous cult experience some years earlier.) So I stayed away for at least a year.

But then a friend gave me a copy of Marion Weinstein's *Positive Magic*, which was so sensible it changed my life forever. I gradually began going to the free "Pagan Way" classes held at Enchantments in the East Village (the original Enchantments on East Ninth Street). There, the basics of casting the Magic Circle were taught. But I chose to proceed very slowly and carefully; I never again wanted to be trapped in a situation from which I couldn't escape. I took my time but came to realize that magic and Wicca (White Witchcraft, the Craft of the Wise) were really geared to the individual, with no group pressure at all. This was good.

I began experimenting with magic. Oh, the fun of it in those early days! Anything was possible. And the enthusiasm of my "beginner's luck" gave me quite a few magical successes right at the start.

My sister was having a difficult time. Her business was slow and she needed to rent her offices; she'd had an ad in *The New York Times* since May and it was now November, with no response. I asked permission to "spiritually help her out" and she agreed.

So I planned a ritual with the proper incense, oil and candle color – all the essential ingredients – and set to work to help my sister. Trying to wait patiently for a few days, I finally called her. You will not believe what she told me: after six months of no response to her ad, the very day after my ritual she rented all her offices and took on three new clients. Wow! I could do magic!

I was so excited that I ran over to Enchantments to tell them about my first major success. I hadn't yet learned – and it's still difficult for me – the importance of Remaining Silent. I bragged about my impressive triumph, only to discover soon after that the new tenant cancelled her check and the new clients cancelled their appointments. My babbling broke the spell. "So much for your spiritual practice," my sister jeered.

Yes, that was quite a lesson. It took me years to learn how to keep my mouth shut, because I'd get so enthusiastic about the amazement of magic that I wanted to tell everybody. (Which is exactly what I'm doing here!) But seriously, I've learned to cool it a little.

After three years of studying magic and the Craft, as it's called, I decided it was time for initiation. Having investigated the world's religions, I had finally found mine and truly loved it. Not knowing a High Priestess I trusted at the time, I decided that self-initiation on the Fall Equinox was the way to go. So with the perfect balance of day and night, light and dark, I took vows to myself and the Gods – and became "Kyler, Priest of Pan, Witch of the Goddess and Magical Man."

The next five years were spent with considerable ups and downs, the misadventures of magical life in New York. On Monday nights I met with a coven for a while and studied privately with an older wisewoman who taught me it's really the *mind* that does magic, all incense, candles and oils merely being aids to inspire the mind. But eventually I realized I had to do things my own way and create my own system. Having pretty much absorbed the knowledge of the Craft, I turned to the Kabbalah, the magical core of Judaism, an infinite study. Tired of people's reactions to the word "witch," I began calling myself a magician, which was becoming more and more true. Being a stickler for perfection, as magicians often are, I chose to work alone, combining elements of Kabbalah and Craft, High and Low Magic. When asked what my magical tradition was, I'd say, "The Kyler Tradition."

By now the substantial results of my magic could no longer be attributed to coincidence. After a healing, a friend with AIDS was able to ride his bike for the first time in a year; after a money spell, $1800 mysteriously appeared in my bank account; after a love ritual, I enjoyed my first relationship in quite a while. But these effects were temporary: my friend got sick again, the $1800 disappeared, and of course the relationship ended. What was *lasting*, though, was the daily work on *myself*, the higher magic that was making me strong.

I began meeting other magicians at the Gnostic Masses given by the OTO (Ordo Templi Orientis), Crowley's magical fraternity. Crowley has always been for me the most brilliant writer on magic; and his Gnostic Mass the most sublime worship service I've ever known. After my cult experience, I'd been very wary of groups, but I really liked the people at OTO, and they seemed to be true to their one law: "Do What Thou Wilt." Unlike the dogmatic cult, this was a philosophy for the individual, called Thelema, which means "Will" in Greek. Some of my heroes were considered saints in the Gnostic Mass: Nietzsche, Wagner – even Moses. So I decided to take the preliminary initiation of Minerval (Zero Degree), which was pretty exciting.

Meanwhile, my psychic counseling practice was growing; and as a new Minerval, I acquired a column in a popular magazine, which catapulted my career.

When I'd been a Minerval for three years, a total of eleven on the Magical Path, I felt ready for further initiation. After a painstaking decision process, I decided against advancing in the OTO, not because I didn't love it, but because of my leftover hesitancy to join any group. Instead, my dear friend and High Priestess, Rozelisa, agreed to initiate me privately into the Gardnerian Tradition of Wicca.

So I finally got my First Degree after eleven years. First Degree in any system is considered a rebirth and you can cast an astrological chart for the special occasion. Although I'm pledged to secrecy, I'm able to say that it was like five years of therapy in one night. I was amazed at how healthy it was; therapists would recommend it, I'm sure, if they knew what it entailed. But they'd have to become witches to find out!

So I now have three major initiations and I wouldn't trade them for anything. They've given me my life, my work, and most importantly, my love for myself. When I told the head of the London OTO that I was only a Minerval, he surprisingly replied that degrees are for those who need them, that some people have them naturally. Yes, I think I've been blessed with that; I've always been a natural for magic. Every fairy tale symbolizes what it's really about: the hero's journey and struggle through life to awaken his Sleeping Beauty, the beauty that lies asleep in his consciousness; and to conquer the obstacles to it with the Mighty Sword of Truth, his mind.

ACTOR TURNED PSYCHIC

> Only your own deep need to salvage something
> from the void – to act or to write or to create – can
> keep you from the commonplace and from dying
> out....Be careful what happens to your talent.
> – Stella Adler

Let's start out with a juicy magical story. During my woebegone days as an actor, I tried to do a lot of magic to help my obstructed career. But short of black magic, there's only so much you can do if something's not meant to be. In *Rosemary's Baby*, John Cassavetes gets the part because the other actor goes blind from black magic. Well, my magic doesn't work that way. And while we're on the subject, those were satanists in *Rosemary's Baby* – NOT witches. Hollywood has been particularly damaging to the true witch's reputation.

But here's the best magic I ever succeeded in doing for my acting career. Having worked with the planets and gods that represent them, I'd had very good luck with Jupiter, who rules the Wheel of Fortune card in the Tarot. So I planned a rite of Jupiter to try to create some good fortune in my career. But after an elaborate ritual, nothing seemed to be happening. Now much of my magic is with seven-day candles; I'm quite good at this, if I do say so myself – but it was the last day of the candle – and nothing. Was it because my neighbors had been so noisy during the ritual? That must have been it.

That day I was doing extra work on the film, *Quiz Show*. I remember seeing my dwindling purple candle as I left my apartment at the ungoddessly hour of 5 A.M. "Come on candle, do something!" I cried. Well, my day turned out to be every extra's dream: I happened to be standing in the right place at the right time and got upgraded to Day Player. Robert Redford, the director, approved my saying four lines. Guess what the Kabbalistic number of Jupiter is: four! I returned home after signing the contract and (the only time this has happened) the glass of my finished candle had shattered! It turns out my scene was cut from the movie, but I still get residual checks to this day.

And that, folks, is the best thing I can tell you about my former acting career.

Oh, extra work: I remember it well. At first it was exciting to hang out on film sets with the stars; but after a few months of making your living this way – and realizing that you're not exactly doing what Stella Adler trained you to do – the tedium sets in big time. I've always been good at making the best of situations and found a wonderful way to deal with all those hours of waiting: to practice Tarot reading with my newly acquired Tarot deck.

Now learning cards is somewhat like learning lines: you can't really act until you've put down the script. Similarly, you can't really read the Tarot until you've weaned yourself off the instruction book. I noted the parallel and one day bravely left my instruction book at home.

The results were astronomical: I achieved the popularity I had always dreamed of in high school! Everyone wanted a reading and no one wanted to go to the set. I was able to unite factions of competitive and jealous actors, everyone truly interested in the intricacies of each other's lives. (Those were the days I used to allow people to listen in; today my readings are strictly private.) I discovered that reading cards became a good way to get out of myself, the self-involved actor; and perhaps for the first time, I began being interested in other people.

Having studied magic for several years, I soon realized that the Tarot encompassed the same forces (of earth, air, fire and water, for instance); but instead of thrusting these forces into action, as one does in magic, I simply interpreted their influence on people's circumstances in life. My accuracy was astonishing, even to me. And almost everyone agreed that I should do it professionally. What? And give up my childhood dream of the stage and screen and bright lights? Never!

One day I was called to the set in the middle of a reading. I sat at a bar with a young woman who asked if I brought my cards with me. When I said no, she handed me her watch and said, "Here – see what you get from this." What follows is my first experience doing psychometry:

I held the watch to my head and immediately got an image, but said, "I can't say this. It's too embarrassing." She said, "It's OK – just say it." I replied, "I really don't think I can." "C'mon," she persisted, "we're all actors." I said, "All right, you have a vaginal yeast infection, don't you?" "Oh my God," she exclaimed, "I can't believe it! I do! What else do you get?" I continued concentrating and said, "You're very uptight about having sex with your boyfriend this weekend." She said, "How true! But *not* because of the yeast infection. Go on." I said, "The reason is because he's impotent." And I was right.

I began to realize that I was truly becoming psychic – but where did this power come from?

The "wisewoman" mentioned in the previous chapter got me started on a daily regimen of exercises for my balance and protection. She warned me that the forces of magic could be very powerful and that I'd better proceed safely. I had read these exercises in *Modern Magick* by Donald Michael Kraig. They included the Lesser Banishing Ritual of the Pentagram, the Banishing Ritual of the Hexagram, and the Middle Pillar Ritual. I began doing these twice daily. They filled me with light and strength.

Stella used to tell us that Stanislavsky, the great Russian director, worked on his voice until the day he died. But as an actor, I hated my vocal exercises; as a psychic and magician, though, I love my magical exercises and will probably do them until the day *I* die. (Or maybe even after I die!) And I believe that the discipline of these exercises inadvertently made me psychic.

Here's how I found out. I was spending a weekend in Massachusetts at the home of an older Jewish man who was dying. One morning I asked if he'd like to witness my Kabbalistic exercises; I thought he might enjoy them because of their Hebrew content. He said he would love to, and his huge dog joined us.

My eyes were mostly closed during the fifteen minutes of the exercises, but I could hear the dog moving around quite a bit – and when I finished and opened my eyes, this enormous dog was at my feet, lying on her back with her legs – and tongue – in the air, panting in total ecstasy! The old man said she had never done this before and that her head had whirled around and around, watching all the swirling lights surrounding me. He then described the three colors of the light: white, blue, and gold, which was absolutely correct!

This proved to me for the first time the validity of a very important magical concept: first you begin *by imagining* a blue pentagram, or a golden hexagram, or a white beam of light. But as you advance in magic, they are no longer imagined; they are truly there. And this man and dog could see them! (Obviously, the man was spiritually advanced; he told me later about his two near-death experiences.)

That was a profound day for me magically. I learned that the light I was bringing down into my head and body was truly entering me. And it was this light from my higher self, my Higher Genius – and beyond – that was making me psychic.

There are so many stories from those early days but a few stand out in my mind. My favorite is when I held a woman's ring and got a cat named "Boots" and "Jesse, the Cool Cat." This sounded so silly, I thought I was making it up. But 3 months later, her California friend moved in with a Jesse and told her, "Jesse named our new cat Boots because of his two booty paws and now he's so pleased, he's going around calling himself Jesse, the Cool Cat!" The woman almost dropped dead on the spot but survived to tell me the tale.

Once I was flying to London on my first non-smoking flight. (When asked if an actor should give up smoking, Stella once said, "Dahling, if you don't smoke, you'll drink!") So due to my lack of puffing, I accidentally overdid it in the booze department and got totally smashed. The man sitting next to me struck up a conversation and asked what I did for a living. When I told him I was becoming a psychic, he confessed that he didn't believe in such things. So I offered him a free demonstration:

I held his ring and got a girl named Maria with blond hair. He said this was his daughter and that she was sitting several rows ahead. Well that was fine, so I tried his other ring and got a Friedrich who was very sad. He told me that Friedrich was his son who had a very unhappy situation occurring in his life – and that he was sitting right next to Maria. This time *I* was the one who said, "I don't believe you!" So he fetched his attaché case from above and showed me two passports with the names "Maria" and "Friedrich." Another skeptic turned believer, with me under the influence, no less.

There's nothing wrong with being a skeptic: show me a hard-boiled skeptic and I'll show you a good egg whose shell can come off. Like the time a young man handed me his bracelet with that defiant look in his eyes. I held the bracelet to my head and said, "I'm getting a Frank… Mesa." He said his best friend was Frank. I said, "So what? Frank could be anyone." He countered, "Well, I was thinking, if you don't say my best friend Frank, I'm not going to believe any of this." But what about Mesa? The next day he called to say he spoke to Frank, who revealed his mother's maiden name: Mesa!

So skeptics, I've got one thing to say to you: BEWARE.

Years ago, while working as a chauffeur, Mike Nichols told me that good actors were a dime a dozen. I think I was a good actor but I was never the right type: I was either too young or too old, too Jewish or too not-Jewish-enough, too good-looking or too not-good-looking-enough. After twenty years, I had had it. I don't think I'd ever have "given up," though, if I hadn't found something else that I loved. And good psychics are not a dime a dozen!

On the set of "Guiding Light" I did some psychometry for one of my fellow extras. I got a Natasha with long, black hair. He said, "Thanks for reminding me – I've been meaning to call her all day." I jokingly added, "You call her Boris, don't you? Just kidding." He said, "No – I really do call her Boris! You're good – you should write a psychic column somewhere." I responded with, "Naaah." But a few weeks later he was selling advertising for a magazine called VICE – and they called to offer me a column.

So I became a psychic columnist. And I soon got the idea to visit one of the restaurants advertised in the magazine to see if they'd like to have a Tarot reader on weekends. The manager was an English bloke who loved the idea. So during the week I continued my battle for acting, but on weekends I started making my first money as a psychic.

I did quite well. And the more disgusted I became with Show Business, the more encouraged I became with my psychic work. I knew if I could find a few restaurants and work four to five nights a week, I could make a decent living at it.

Which is just what I did. A red Mars candle led me to my best gig ever at Caffé Sha Sha in the West Village; and VICE Magazine led to the very popular NEXT Magazine, which brought lots of people into Caffé Sha Sha to see me. I was on my way.

What a crazy life it is being a psychic! People expect perfection; they think I should know everything. And I don't – I only know what comes to me through the cards and my psychic messages. I don't claim to be 100% accurate (well, maybe 99%!), but I *do* try to be 100% honest. And I think my clients appreciate that; it's so rewarding to be able to help them in a deep way.

But God, the flack I have to take sometimes! I've heard every psychic joke in the book and some can be downright nasty. Let's face it: I'm not in a very respected profession. What's difficult for me is that I get super-sensitive when doing a reading – that's part of my talent for it. So sometimes the "vulgarity of the public" really gets to me. I have to remember to keep my sense of humor.

It's thrilling, though, to have so many wonderful clients. I never thought it could happen. Much to my own amazement, they return again and again, telling me how my predictions came true. I always maintain, however, that the future is never as important as one's understanding of the *present* (from which we create our future).

Every once in a while, I get a real stinker. One of my worst experiences early on was a woman who wanted to know when her former psychiatrist was going to call, because she just *knew* he was in love with her and seven other psychics said he would call in February. Well, February was almost over and the cards were terrible. So I said, "I'm sorry, I don't think he's going to call you." Then she stood up and announced in a very loud voice: "I DON'T LIKE THIS READING!"

One of my most uncomfortable experiences was with a woman who lived in my building. The session started out great: when I got the name Fantine from her ring (the character from *Les Misérables*), she said that her boyfriend left her for the woman who was playing the role on Broadway. I thought the rest of the session was OK, but for a whole year she gave me the gloomiest looks in the elevator. Finally I asked her about it and she said that *nothing* I predicted came true! I felt awful because I'm such a perfectionist. So I offered her a free reading but she never showed up.

Maybe I was off, but I've learned from experience that people don't always take my advice; I'm a psychic *counselor* – so if someone doesn't choose the job I highly recommend, and stays with the one he hates instead, then he won't have the fabulous summer I predicted – which is exactly what happened to one of my clients.

But thank God, the exasperating experiences are relatively few. My work is constantly amazing; and no one is more amazed than I.

There's a beautiful play I saw years ago about a man so in love with his childhood sweetheart that he follows her all over the world – only to discover one day that he's much better suited to her older sister, whom he marries in the end. It haunted me at the time, wondering if I was chasing after the wrong dream. But over the years, one dream simply vaporized into another dream. And I cry as I write this, for I realize that it's all really the same dream: it's about finding the life that you love.

TAROT AND I CHING – KEYS TO SELF-KNOWLEDGE

When there are things to do, one can become great.
Hence there follows the hexagram of APPROACH.
Approach means becoming great.

– *I Ching*, Wilhelm/Baynes translation

When I was taking the Pagan Way class mentioned in "Adventures on the Magical Path," I swore I'd never get a Tarot deck. How could I possibly learn the meanings of 78 cards? Besides, I was using the more respected and scholarly *I Ching*, which fulfilled all my divination needs. Everyone else did Tarot, but I was the *I Ching* mavin – so I thought I'd leave it at that.

But when someone from the class gave me a reading with his Barbara Walker Tarot deck, I was intensely attracted to the beauty of the cards. For two weeks I resisted my desire to purchase them for myself, but I finally succumbed.

It's simply not true that it's "bad luck" to buy your own deck. There are so many superstitions surrounding the occult – and they're all nonsense. I try to weed every superstition out of my work; I choose to keep it practical, scientific and down-to-earth. I've purchased both of my decks and they've brought me nothing but "good luck."

Funny that my two decks, the Barbara Walker and Aleister Crowley decks, are both intensely dramatic in different ways. (I wasn't voted "most dramatic" in high school for nothing.) These are the only two I use: the smaller Walker deck for traveling to my restaurants, clients' houses and parties; and the larger Crowley deck for my private clients at home, where it rests in my "magic drawer" with my other tools. Both serve me well.

I've chosen to read surprisingly little on the Tarot. One accompanying book per deck is about all. I think it's important for the symbolism to come from a deep place within – and not to be infused with too many outside ideas and words. So Walker's *Secrets of the Tarot*, Crowley's *Book of Thoth*, and later Dion Fortune's *Mystical Qabalah* are about all I'd recommend.

The whole universe is contained in the Tarot: the ancient wisdom of the ages and the deep fathoms of the subconscious mind are all hidden within it. The more you use it, the more you become aware of its depth and sublimity. It just keeps growing.

At first you begin by reading for yourself, of course. And there's nothing wrong with that; in fact, when you're learning, it's a very good tool to help you know yourself. But eventually it's wise to practice on friends (or if you can do extra work…!) because you can't in all actuality read for yourself. Others may disagree, but I recommend the *I Ching* for individual use and maintain that the Tarot can actually be deceiving for oneself, because you can manipulate the cards subconsciously and can't really interpret them objectively. This doesn't mean not to do it, especially while you're learning. I still read for myself all the time, but I don't trust it the way I do with my clients. If the cards were true for myself, I'd be having one love affair after another with everyone who tickles my fancy – and in reality this is very far from the truth!

For me, there were two levels of learning the cards, represented by my two decks. The first was a simpler, Wiccan approach (Walker), and the second, a more advanced Kabbalistic approach (Crowley). As with my magic, I now combine both approaches. But this takes time. It's best to begin at the beginning.

The four suits: cups, pentacles, wands and swords, correspond to the hearts, diamonds, clubs and spades of modern playing cards. They represent the four elements, the four directions and four magical tools. Cups (hearts) represent water and west – love and emotion; pentacles (diamonds), earth and north – money, the physical plane; wands (clubs), fire and south – the will; and swords (spades), air and east – the mind. Sounds a bit like bridge, doesn't it? Just as complicated: if only I had known what I was getting into!

The Tarot cards were the forerunners of modern playing cards. The early Christian priests edited many of the cards out of the deck because of their "sinful" nature. All the princesses were banished (too many attractive young ladies) and all the major cards were deleted, except for the unthreatening Fool, who became the Joker. The 21 other major cards were considered the Devil's work. They had to go, as did all natural pagan expression. By using them today, we are truly dealing with the primal power of human consciousness.

So we have 22 Major Arcana cards, which represent major archetypal situations in life; we have 16 Court Cards representing people and elemental combinations; and we have 40 Minor Arcana cards for smaller, specific ideas.

Are you ready to do a reading? Pick out one card, if you've got a deck, and respond to the picture. Your response is much more important than what any book says. Eventually, of course, one has to have the knowledge of the cards – and then balance this knowledge with intuition. If you can put together the left-brain Apollonian knowledge with the right-brain Dionysian intuition, you might become a powerful reader. Every art form has its technique plus its feeling or talent; and every artist must combine the two to produce a work of art, whether it be a painting, a symphony or a Tarot reading.

Let's suppose you've chosen the 3 of Cups, a damn good card. So good, in fact, they named a restaurant in New York after it. Barbara Walker calls it "Grace" and Crowley calls it "Abundance." On the former we see three women joyously lifting each of their cups up high; and on the latter we see three red-jeweled goblets, overflowing with water. How would you respond to this? You might get the idea of a happy celebration, which is what I sometimes say.

There's a funny story I have with the 3 of Cups. When it appeared in readings with the Walker deck, I noticed that it often implied love triangles. Again and again this seemed to be true. Once I was reading the female bartender at Stingy Lulu's in the East Village, where I used to read cards. She was asking me about her boyfriend. Well, the 3 of Cups showed up and I was immediately inspired to say, "The two of you are going to have a *ménage à trois*." She responded, "That's impossible – he's too square – it could never happen." But one week later, as soon as I entered the front door, she ran over to me and exclaimed, "Kyler! You were right! We had a *ménage à trois*!"

That's my 3 of Cups story; but every card has its own story – and it's up to you to discover what they are for *you*.

The Tarot and *I Ching* work on the principle of synchronicity, Carl Jung's term for meaningful coincidence. The cards (or coins) that appear in their specific places have meaning. And I've devised my own method of shuffling and cutting that works like a miracle every time. In "Actor Turned Psychic," I said that I don't claim to be 100% accurate; actually, I was referring to the future. But with my method, the *present* is nearly 100% accurate, so much so that I can describe any situation with near-total accuracy because of the way the cards appear. It's really uncanny. My confidence in this is so strong, that if a client denies what I'm saying about the present, I've been known to say, "I beg to differ." And my insistence on the truth as I see it is usually correct. That's how accurate the cards are.

The future is a different story; it's definitely subject to change with a multitude of factors influencing it. I've heard it said that the best psychics guess at the future. Maybe so, but the present is almost always on target.

You may ask, "Well, what do I need to know the present for?" A good question. As a psychic counselor, I'm interested in showing why a situation is what it is, with all its psychological ramifications, so that you'll have a deeper understanding of it before we move on to the future. Also, it's important that I impress you at the beginning of a reading so that you'll trust me for its duration.

Now I work differently than most readers do; my approach is unique. I interpret everything that happens during a reading, not just the cards: the music that's playing, a glass that crashes, etc. Although I don't actually do magic during a reading, I bring "light" into my clients – maybe that's why they feel so good when they're sitting there – and incorporating the three phases of the moon, I say a prayer to insure that the cards are perfect. I don't use the popular Rider-Waite deck or the famous Celtic Cross spread. I don't do general readings – I think they're too vague – and I don't believe in reversed cards. Finally, I don't place dozens of cards on the table – only a specific few: I've got a lot to say about each one.

As one gets more advanced with the cards, a study of the Kabbalah is essential. True, there are many ways to interpret the Tarot – and most "fortune tellers" know nothing about the Kabbalah; yet the similarity of the cards to the Kabbalistic Tree of Life is simply too striking to ignore. For example, there are 22 Hebrew letters, 22 Major Arcana cards and 22 pathways on the Tree of Life. They all fit together. The pathways connect ten spheres representing ace through ten, each having a divine emanation, from the planets down to the earth-plane. A fascinating, intricate study – and many readers know nothing about it!

I could talk forever about the cards and how to read them; but I'll leave the choice of this pursuit to you. So let's conclude with this advice: study the cards less and study life more. Open your eyes to every occurrence, every omen that is sent your way. There is meaning everywhere – and remember, there are no "coincidences." Learn about the arts. Learn about psychology. Discover all of life.

What's so remarkable about the *I Ching* (Book of Changes) is that it does it all for you. You just have to know the simple technique of tossing the coins. If I could have only one book on a desert island, it would be my beloved *I Ching*, as long as I could have three pennies in my bathing suit pocket. I've had very few teachers on the Magical Path; and through thick and thin, the *I Ching* has been my teacher.

Predating Confucius, the book is a font of ancient Chinese wisdom, praised highly by Jung and used daily by Crowley. You toss three coins six times and look up the answer. Jung's principle of synchronicity works the same here as with the Tarot. There is nothing I could recommend more confidently. Not only is it easy to use, but every time a question is asked, you receive a dose of excellent philosophy with the answer. Simply amazing, always ennobling, it teaches us how to be "superior" men and women.

Like the Tarot, it deals with elements of nature, only different ones: heaven, earth, lake, water, wind, fire, thunder and mountain. The toss of the coins makes a "secret code" that determines these elements. In different combinations, through 64 hexagrams, they imply the many situations of life.

You've simply got to try it for yourself. I recommend the Wilhelm/ Baynes translation. You might need a dictionary, but it's worth it; it's the definitive version. Richard Wilhelm, an *I Ching* expert, translated the original Chinese into German; and Cary F. Baynes rendered it into English. Jung wrote the well-known foreword to this edition, which can be found in any bookstore.

Jung says it's rare for the book *not* to give an amazing answer. That's true. Often the answer contains the same words as your question. The one time I was attacked in New York (from behind), the *I Ching* told me soon after the fact: "If one is not extremely careful, somebody may come up from behind and strike [you]. Misfortune." I wished I had consulted the oracle before the attack! (Note: Wanting to give the exact wording of this quotation, I had no idea where in the book to find it. I told myself to simply open it at random and that I'd hit the exact page – and guess what: I did. Coincidence?)

After years of consulting the oracle – and of course, the real oracle is your subconscious mind – I've come to expect answers that are truly on-the-mark and have learned to trust it. But when you first begin, you'll be dumbfounded by the way it speaks to you. It really seems to prove that something "cosmic" is going on out there, when a few coins can lead to such enlightening words, almost always on the exact subject you've chosen.

But aside from the fun of it, there's an important reason for using the *I Ching* – and I recommend using it daily. The reason is that it lifts you. It wants you to be a "superior" person, the best you can be, rising high above anything "inferior." It wants you to attain your stature in life. It scorns pettiness and deceit. It encourages all noble virtues. It criticizes you when you've been small-minded and praises you when you've been wise. It leads you, like the songbird in Wagner's *Siegfried*, to the mountain of fire, your Higher Genius, where you'll ignite the heroic in you – and achieve your destiny in this world.

THE POTENTIAL FOR GENIUS

[The man of] talent is like the marksman who hits a target that others cannot reach; [the] genius is like the marksman who hits a target...[the] others cannot even see.

– Schopenhauer

In the musical version of J.M. Barrie's *Peter Pan*, when Peter tells Wendy she's "just too grown-up" to return to Neverland, what he really means is that she's lost her artist's soul. In our society, most of us lose this soul, while as children we have it naturally and are encouraged to have it. Peter Pan is the Eternal Artist, the God and Goddess, the genius. He flies high above the world, defying even gravity. He teaches others to fly, but they have to believe in magic, in fairies – in *themselves* – in order to do so.

Peter Pan is profoundly lonely. Most other children grow up and join society; they learn to conform to the sensible ways of adults. When Captain Hook asks, "Pan, what art thou?" Peter proclaims: "I am youth! I am joy! I am freedom!" He is truly mythic, representing the Great God Pan in human form. He alone knows the way to Neverland, which is the secret Magic Circle, beyond all time and space.

Sometimes when flying within my own Magic Circle, I experience an intense déjà vu of when I was a boy, dancing around our dark basement to the fantasy music of *Peter Pan* with only a flashlight for the stars. I may have been Peter then, but I'm certainly Pan now!

Which leads us to the delicate and controversial subject of genius. At the climax of Ionesco's play, *Rhinoceros*, when everyone else in the world has turned into the animal of the title, the hero Berenger unlocks his liquor cabinet and surrenders to his favorite bottle of brandy. As a testament to his individuality, he faces the audience and toasts: "I'm the last man left, and I'm staying that way until the end. I'm not capitulating!" And he drinks as the curtain falls.

What is being said here about the artist, the individual, the genius? Well, for one thing, that it ain't easy! Stella Adler used to say, "Never psychoanalyze the artist." What she meant was: don't label him (or her) an alcoholic, a narcissist, an obsessive-compulsive. The life of the artist, the genius, is the struggle to triumph over the confines – and cruelty – of society; and to do so at all cost. How can we judge the life of a "sensitive" genius like Tennessee Williams, Kurt Cobain or Sarah Kane, the late English playwright, by saying that their excesses led them to their doom? Or how can we condemn the life of a "brutal" genius like Picasso, Wagner or Crowley, when they fought to leave us such great bodies of work?

In *Surviving Picasso*, the Merchant/Ivory film, Anthony Hopkins struts across the screen like Shaw's Superman, like Crowley's Man of Will. Beyond morality, Hopkins' Picasso is one with art. To do, to will, to paint. And to make love! Nietzsche said, "Whatever is done from love always occurs beyond good and evil." This is the driving force of the artist.

Prejudice, incidentally, is the opposite of art. It's a narrowing of the higher faculties. There's "positive" prejudice: the maitre d' at La Goulue restaurant said, "We have the best *frites* in New York." (Which perhaps is true.) And there's "negative" prejudice: the subtle bigotry of racism, anti-Semitism, homophobia.

Prejudice always stems from a narrow way of seeing. "You've got to be carefully taught," wrote Oscar Hammerstein. Art, on the other hand, comes from an opening of consciousness – beyond mind, beyond judgment – and beyond fear or jealousy, which is what prejudice is really about.

Great art calls to us to be bigger than ourselves. That's why the art of a nation is the soul of a nation. And art will always beckon to us to rise above our prejudices – to see the world from a higher perspective, a perspective of love (Ace of Cups) over fear or cruelty (Nine of Swords).

The genius is the individual who brings this art to the world.

The Age of Aquarius, the astrological sign of genius, has begun to bloom. At last, we are no longer "dawning." What does this mean? Well, first of all, it means that the religions of the former Piscean Age, founded on sin and archaic laws, have become passé. It's time to celebrate the new spirituality, where religion and science converge. Einstein said, "Science without religion is blind; religion without science is lame." He was obviously ahead of his time. The religions of the Piscean Age negated science; the religions of the Aquarian Age will confirm science. And the genius will triumph as his own God.

More and more, scientists and physicists acknowledge what ancient religions always knew about magic and psychic phenomena. The relationship between spirit and matter, between the psychic and the mundane, is being recognized as something tangible and scientific. We're beginning to realize that *we* are the masters, that God is not an all-powerful bearded man in heaven, but instead a power within each one of us. Yes, there's a "cosmic energy" that you could call God, but what's significant is the magical link that every human being can make with this energy.

From personal experience, I can assure you, it's real. It's exciting. It's the way we're going. Now I'm an Aquarius, so why take my word for it? All I can say is you'll see: we're finally in the Aquarian Age – let's wake up to reality!

Once I attended a performance of Philip Glass's *The Voyage* at the Metropolitan Opera. I've always considered Philip Glass, the Aquarian composer, to be a visionary artist. And his iconoclastic opera got me thinking about the nature of genius. So without further introduction, here are some ideas on GENIUS VERSUS SOCIETY:

1. We all have the potential for genius.
2. A genius is someone who succeeds in making contact with his/her higher self, Higher Genius, or Holy Guardian Angel.
3. A person who is in touch with his/her genius is totally individual.
4. Stella Adler, also an Aquarius, made her students promise to take all "indication" out of their work. Indication in acting or any art form is the hinting at genius, copying it without experiencing it.
5. If one is not expressing his genius, his individuality, then his expression, in art or in life, comes out as cliché.
6. The alternative to genius is society, the middle class.
7. "The artist is the highest class," Stella used to say.

8. Society is threatened by the genius, though greatly enriched by him/her.
9. Society insists on conformity and is therefore the greatest enemy to the genius.
10. The genius tears down society.
11. The number of genius, the number of Aquarius, the number of magical power.

It suddenly occurs to me that I'd better address the subject of how the author views himself in this area, lest he be accused of having secret (or overt) hubris beyond belief. Let me try to be as honest as I can about this. Years ago, someone said that my eyes see more than they can handle. I think this was true at the time. And although I can be so thick in some ways, I was told by the best psychic I ever met, the late Clifford Bias, that I'm "near genius" and "the best attitude is to kid about it," otherwise I might be considered a "conceited ass."

Thinking this was good advice, I tried to take myself less seriously, but it took a long time to develop a sense of humor about myself. Once, while chauffeuring Jackie Onassis, I found her lost umbrella on Madison Avenue. "You're a genius!" she cooed. That was during my acting days; but more recently, at least two people have told me that I have a genius for reading the cards.

This may be true, but I really think it's the work that counts. People don't realize the work I do at night to be able to read their cards in the day. I work harder than most people I know – and always have. "A" was never good enough for me; it had to be "A-plus." Maybe I was trying to please my father or my mother or whatever; but for me the "plus" was always the magic, like the glitter on a magical candle: not at all necessary, but oh, so dazzling. I worked for the "plus."

When I'm writing, I work all day and all night. It's an intense, grueling process: the work just takes over, like a fever. Sometimes I wake up with my latest chapter in bed in the morning. My work is my lover; I'm devoted to my work. I've always been this way: I have to give the very best that's in me.

Whether this makes me a genius or not, I don't know. But I *do* know what Irene Bertuzzi, a flamboyant palm reader in Italy, told me when I was 17: "Your life line and your work line intersect: your life and your work are one. Your father goes to the office and leaves his work at the end of the day. But you, Jimmy (my childhood name) – you *will succeed! Because you can do it! You have it in you!* But you will have to go through so much pain first…because you are so sensitive: I can see it in your eyes."

That was the summer of 1970: Porto Santo Stefano, Italy. They were playing Led Zeppelin's "Whole Lotta Love" – and I was about to be a senior in high school. I thought the sensitivity in my eyes would make me a famous actor; little did I realize that it would be the way I'd make my living: a "sensitive" is another word for a "psychic."

I've tried to be honest about how I personally relate to the subject of genius. So now we can proceed, finally, and focus on *you*: the person with the potential for something great.

The first principle on my eleven-point list was "We all have the potential for genius." OK, I've said it; but now you've got to do the work.

In his excellent book, *Young Nietzsche: Becoming a Genius*, Carl Pletsch asserts that geniuses are made, not born. I tend to agree. Pletsch says: "In his struggle to please Wagner, Nietzsche discovered his own creativity and learned many of the psychological characteristics of genius: audacity, narcissism, and single-mindedness. Eventually he would be able to practice these virtues of genius."

Are you ready to practice the "virtues of genius?" Not if you believe in a "selfless" philosophy or religion. There's no mincing words here: to be a genius, to accomplish something extraordinary, you've got to practice "selfishness." Let's not obliterate the self, the ego, too quickly on our spiritual paths. If we sit around meditating on a mountain somewhere, we might attain the Buddhist "no mind," but we certainly won't design that palatial estate, erect that superlative sculpture, or shoot the film that will influence people around the world.

The choice is yours; this is not a chapter – or book – about enlightenment. This is a chapter about achievement. Are you ready to achieve something in your life? If so, you have to figure out what that is. And then you've got to fight for it!

If you choose what Crowley calls your "True Will," then the doors of life will open fairly quickly and naturally on your chosen path. It's amazing how the universe helps us when we're doing the "right thing," and how it socks us in the jaw when we're not. (See the movie *Run Lola Run*.)

So first you need to discover where your potential for genius lies. It may not be where you think it is. The espresso maker at Caffé Sha Sha several years ago was obviously unhappy with his job. His coffee wasn't the greatest, but every Friday, when he purchased the flowers for the weekend, his floral arrangements were unbelievable. I tried to encourage him to do this kind of work for a living, but he wasn't interested. Some people just love to be miserable.

Has anyone ever told you that you have a genius for something? A genius for flowers, or a genius for people, or a genius for cars or for picking out the best hat? Comments like these are clues that we probably *do* have genius in these areas. And I believe that we all need to get in touch with the genius part of ourselves, to begin utilizing it 150%, and to make a lot of money doing it! Unless you prefer to meditate on top of a mountain – and maybe *that's* your True Will, which is fine.

But whatever your will in life is – get *to* it, get *on* it, and *get going*! If you choose the mountain, then go find it and stop dreaming about it. But if you choose the work, if you choose greatness, if you choose any of the arts – it's got to be the number one choice in your life. There's simply no compromise with this: genius is something you work for. You can't have it two ways; as I tried to tell a friend, choose either the New Jersey family life or a great career in the theatre – but "You can't have both, dahling," as Stella often reminded us. There are exceptions, of course, but they're exceedingly rare.

Are you ready to take the leap and pursue something magnificent in your life? You've got to do it with your blood, your guts – every ounce of your being. And there's no guarantee that you'll ever "make it." The only guarantee is that you'll discover who you are.

At the climax of *Peter Pan*, Tiger Lilly decrees: "Peter Pan is the sun and the moon and the stars! Peter Pan is the love of delight! Peter Pan is the bravest and strongest of all boys!" And Peter answers, "Yes, I know. I don't say it to boast – it's because I cannot tell a lie."

The genius doesn't need to lie; his life and work tell the truth.

INTERNATIONAL
PSYCHIC

Do you believe that psychic energy is transmitted from person to person only in close proximity? (Or do you believe in psychic phenomena at all?) Well, here's a story proving that psychic vibes can travel overseas.

During my last trip to England, I visited the Warburg Institute at the University of London. It's very difficult to gain access there; you need a special reason to enter. I was determined, as usual, and succeeded in convincing the strict librarians on the importance of my mission. Within the secret confines of the institute are hidden many documents, letters and manuscripts of the late Aleister Crowley, the great magical genius of the 20th Century.

Initially I was disappointed because the 78 original paintings of the Crowley Tarot Deck were under lock-and-key; no one was allowed to see them due to some publisher's dispute. But the material I eventually held in my hands was the highlight of my trip.

There were original letters to Crowley from the likes of Dion Fortune (another great writer/occultist), Somerset Maugham and the sculptor Rodin, who wrote dozens of letters. There were magical diaries, scrapbooks, original manuscripts (including the sublime *Liber Aleph*, hand-written in red ink) and many sensationalized press clippings. I thought, "If the folks in New York could see this!"

After returning home, I went straight to Enchantments (the original

Enchantments), my favorite magical shop, to tell what I'd seen. Carol, the owner, happened to be "visible" that day and told me she had just dreamed about an institute with Crowley documents and manuscripts! Although it was a vivid dream, she was puzzled by its meaning.

"When did you have this dream?" I asked. "Tuesday morning around ten," she recalled. "Carol!" I exclaimed, "Add five hours for the time difference and that's exactly when I was there—Tuesday at three!" We howled with amazement, realizing we were involved in a magical connection across the Atlantic Ocean!

WAGNER'S RING AND
THE WIZARD OF OZ

A few years ago, I was invited to the Harvard Club to hear a lecture given by Hildegard Behrens, the soprano, on Wagner's Ring Cycle. To my delight, her approach to the four Ring operas was through the four elements of Astrology, as she called them. You should have seen the looks on those Harvard Club faces as Ms. Behrens elaborated on her thesis! *Das Rheingold*, she said, represents water; *Die Walküre*, air; *Siegfried*, earth; and *Götterdämmerung*, fire. It was wonderful to hear an artist of her stature admit to what is so basic and primal in all the arts.

The four elements are with us always: in the four suits of the Tarot, the four seasons, the four directions, the four movements of a symphony. Anything that exists in a group of four probably has these attributions. *The Wizard of Oz* is my favorite example. Dorothy represents earth (the home, the hearth, the physical), the Scarecrow represents air (the mind, the intellect), the Lion, fire (energy, courage, will) and the Tin Man, water (emotion, the heart). These characters *always* had the qualities of their individual elements—they just needed the Wizard's validation; they needed society's acknowledgment of who they really were.

Isn't that like most of us? We need our diplomas, certificates, licenses, medals and degrees. Without these, who are we? We're naked as air, formless as fire, sinking in water, lost on earth. Oh, the anxiety of it all! That's when we're *truly* free, and that's when we discover the fifth element, the element of spirit. As Paul Tillich said, "The courage to be is rooted in the God who appears when God has disappeared in the anxiety of doubt." There's *The Wizard of Oz* for you.

PART TWO:
FICTION

THE CONSCIOUS
EGOIST

My life was about to be transformed. But I didn't know it yet. How could I? I was sitting in my office, waiting for Jennifer Filenbaum to show up. She was five minutes late and my favorite patient. Of course I never told her this. She was quite funny usually—and I was getting so bored with most of my clientele—sitting and listening to their problems all day. Jennifer was one of the few who made me laugh.

My name is Davis Jarvey and I'm a therapist. A *good* therapist. My patients love me. I help them with their troubles. And I'm really getting sick of it.

I have two outstanding features: my mind and...you can guess the other one. Women used to love it—the other one, I mean. Now men do. No one gives a shit about my mind.

Well, that's not really true. There's at least one person who cares about my mind—my literary agent. You see, I'd written this outrageous novel, THE CONSCIOUS EGOIST, and my agent and I were waiting for about five and a half months to hear from a publisher. If you've never written a book, I'll tell you, it takes a really long time to hear anything. I guess because everyone's so busy reading everyone else's—dare I say it?—crap.

But as I waited for Jennifer, and as I waited to hear from my agent, which I was always doing, we knew it could be any day. Would I stay working as a bored but brilliant therapist for the rest of my life? Or would the publication of THE CONSCIOUS EGOIST catapult me into the soaring heights of glittering acclaim?

The phone rang. Would this be the call to change my life?

It was Jennifer: "Davis—I'm so sorry, but I'm stuck in a taxi and the traffic's not moving! Can we begin the session over the phone?"

"What's the taxi driver's name?" I asked.

"Mohammed Abdul," replied Jennifer.

"And how would you feel," I continued, "about Abdul hearing the intimate details of your love life, or lack of it, Jennifer?"

"How would I feel?"

"That's what I said."

"You're always asking me that, Davis."

"Well, maybe it's time you got in touch with your feelings. Tell Mohammed to get his ass over to Charles Street as fast as he can." And I hung up.

Don't think I'm being cruel here. My supervisor, Nicholas, advised me to be particularly tough with Jennifer because her parents were never tough with her and consequently transformed her into this all-knowing monster, for which she was miserable her whole life long. Should one trust the advice of one's supervisor? One has no choice in therapy land: our supervisors are kings—or queens—as the case may be. And I loved Nicholas; his sessions with me were like heaven; he always confirmed my brilliance, yet dignified his criticism of me with a dagger of nobility from which I emerged unscathed, yet somehow improved—as if improvement were possible in my case.

"Nicholas, where are you now that I need you?" I sighed as I waited by the hung-up receiver for my favorite patient. Jennifer, oh Jennifer, I thought, if only my life could be as pure as yours. If only you knew how neurotic your beloved therapist really was!

My Siamese cat, Alphonse, entered and jumped up on my lap. "What are we going to do, Alphonse," I purred, as I petted him nervously. "The session started five minutes ago—and I've got to stop at ten of three. Will Jennifer understand? Or will she insist on pursuing some new problem discovered precisely at 2:45, just when it's time to leave? Will I have to forcibly remove her, my pet? Perhaps you can help me."

The phone rang. Oh my God—should I answer it? I was, after all, officially in a session. I let the machine get it: "You have reached the office of Davis Jarvey. Please leave a message and I will return your call promptly. Thank you."

It was my agent! "Davis, darling, this is Harriet. Could you please fax me a copy of your *New York Times* interview? I seem to have misplaced it and need another for a new submission. Thanks, love."

Oh, Harriet—I loved her dearly—but she was so unorganized. How did she ever expect to sell my novel? She was driving me crazy. I couldn't stand another day of my exacerbated rage against her. I pushed Alphonse off my lap and went to the john. Some cold water on my face might make me appear calm and collected when Jennifer arrived.

The doorman buzzed. I raced out of the bathroom, towel in hand, and said, "Yes, Mick?"

"It's Jennifer on her way up to see you, Mr. Jarvis."

"That's Jarvey. Davis Jarvey."

"OK, Mr. Jarvey."

"Thank you."

And Jennifer arrived with a flourish and a flutter—blond hair, red dress, green bag—talking a mile a minute, as usual:

"Davis, My God, you wouldn't believe the traffic—you wouldn't believe the day I've had! *Oi Gevalt!* I'm a wreck, a total wreck. I couldn't get the kids to school, I couldn't find a taxi, I couldn't find my diaphragm, not that I have anyone to use it with—but just in case—after the session, you never know—and what am I doing here? *Why am I here?* What can we accomplish today? With just a half hour left practically? I can't take any more of this...I've got to go away on a vacation or something...."

"Jennifer, why don't you come sit down and tell me about it?"

"Do you really care, Davis?" she asked as she chose the chaise lounge for the day's session. "Or is it just a front?"

"Why is it important for you to know that?"

" 'Why,' he asks! 'Why?' I'll tell you why. Because I would like to feel that somebody really cares about me, for once. Do you know what I mean? Do you really care about me, Davis? Or is it just my money you care about?"

"Now Jennifer—these questions don't suit you and you know it. Let's get to the bottom of them. Let's try some free association. I'll say a word and you say the first thing that comes into your mind, OK?"

"All right, but I'm very dubious."

"Well, let's try it...."

"OK," she said, reluctantly.

"Now lean back, close your eyes, and say the first word that comes into your mind."

"OK."

"*Care...*"

"...Nurse."

"*Doctor...*"

"...Penis."

"*Vagina...*"

"...Love."

48

"*Love...*"

"*...Fuck.*"

"*Sex...*"

"*...Death.*"

"*Suicide...*"

"*...Cure.*"

"*Escape...*"

"*...Fuck me!*"

"*Professional...*"

"*...Turn-on.*"

"*Doctor...*"

"*...Penis.*"

"*Nurse...*"

"*...Wants it.*"

"*Why...*"

"*...Emptiness.*"

"*Fulfillment...*"

"...THAT'S IT!!!" she cried. "I've just realized how I substitute my own feelings of inadequacy with the need for a man's cock."

"Very good, Jennifer. I think you were able to release some of your aggressions there. Do you feel better?"

"I do, Davis. You are so good!"

"Thank you."

"Now why don't you tell *me* what's bothering *you* today?"

"How can you tell that something's bothering me?"

"I can tell, Davis—woman's intuition."

"Well, this is your session—so we need to explore your reasons for asking."

"Oh, cut the bull, Davis. We're two human beings relating to each other. I'm paying you, but we're still two human beings—despite your self-assured arrogance, the grim, confident tone in your voice. So what's the matter with you today?"

"Jennifer, we only have fifteen minutes. Are you sure this is how you choose to spend the rest of your session?"

"Yes! I feel released—I feel wonderful. Now I'd like to help you. So tell me."

"That would be highly unprofessional."

"I won't tell anyone. Tell Jennifer your troubles."

"You think I have troubles? Perhaps you're projecting."

"What are you feeling, Davis?"

"Why do want to know this?"

"Maybe I care about you. What are you feeling?"

I took a deep breath.

"What are you feeling?" she asked again.

"I'm feeling...."

"Yes...."

"Sadness...infinite sadness."

"That's an honest answer. Why?"

"Because I've written a book—and it's already been rejected twenty-six times. No one believes in me except my agent; otherwise I am totally alone in this world. This causes me infinite sadness because the day may never come when I'll be recognized for who I am: a man with original ideas—not just a therapist, not just your average professional guy—but a writer, an artist."

"I'm surprised to hear you talk this way," she confessed.

"So am I," I replied. "Shall I continue?"

"Um-hmm," she nodded.

"I've sacrificed everything to try to get what I want—the only thing

I want—to be published, which seems so impossible. Suffering is the only thing that seems possible."

She was silent. And I was growing more and more agitated:

"I've put every ounce of energy into my book—and it's turning my hair gray. I've got circles under my eyes. I haven't had sex since God knows when. Gray hair may be appealing to women in the heterosexual world—but not so with gay men. I'm getting older, Jennifer, and what have I got to show for it? I come from a rich family, you know; sure I make a decent living as a therapist—but until I get that huge advance as a writer, I'm just not in their league. The pressure to succeed in an upper-middle-class family is one of the great pressures of our time. If I don't have a breakdown, I'm afraid I could have a heart attack. It's all about trying to please my father who never gave me any approval."

She was still silent.

"Yet it all comes down to this futile sense of loneliness; the despair of having no relief in sight. I've realized lately that there is only one cure. Not drugs, not drinking, not sex, not meditation, not magic, not getaway trips—only one cure—as hopeless as it may seem. Writing— whether I'm published or not—writing is the only cure...because it makes me conscious of who I am."

After a long pause, she said, "Wow...you know...you really are an egotist, Davis."

"Well, you wanted me to talk about myself, didn't you? But the term is 'egoist'—there is a difference. And I am aware—very aware—of my egoism."

"Well, egoism or egotism—it's all the same to me. Our time is up, Mr. Jarvey. Today and always. I can't believe it, but you are not the man I thought you were. I always thought you were so together. I've got to go now, I'm sorry." And she got up to leave.

51

"Just a minute, Jennifer. You haven't paid me for the session."

"No, I haven't. Apparently, when you get to the heart of what you truly feel, what is truly deep inside you, it's just an embarrassment—and nobody else is interested. It's you who should pay me, sweetheart, for I'm teaching you a major lesson of life: nobody really cares what anyone really feels—unless they're getting paid for it."

And she walked out on me. I never saw the woman again.

I lost most of my patients after that. I didn't want to listen to them anymore; I just wanted to hear myself talk. I was simply the most fascinating character around. You see, no one understood life, the world, the people in it—in short, the Human Condition—better than I. No one had the brains I had—or the size of equipment I had—to bring forth my unique offering of ideas and power to this confused, emasculated world.

The phone rang. I let the machine get it. I was in no mood to talk to anyone.

"You have reached the office of Davis Jarvey. Please leave a message and I will return your call promptly. Thank you."

"Davis! This is Harriet!"

She sounded drunk.

"Great news, darling! You won't believe it—we sold the book! Finally! We got an offer of seventeen thousand from Bad Boy Books in L.A! I had to fuck that editor senseless! Call me right away, Davis! Bye, honey!"

What did I just hear? Was I losing my mind? I went to the machine to listen to the message again...but as I reached for the button, I started feeling dizzy and nauseous. I thought I was going to throw up. It felt like everything was spinning...and I fell down and passed out. Unconscious, devoid of awareness, I lay on my thick, orange carpet in total oblivion....

I must have come to about an hour later. The only thing I remember is the feeling of Alphonse licking my face with his hard, prickly tongue—a coarse reminder of reality.

I was conscious once again and ready for my new life.

THE LONELIEST MAN
ON EARTH

I've got a story to tell. There's a problem though—already, so soon—and that is: I don't know the story. I don't have any ideas. I don't know what's going to happen in the story and I don't know who I, the narrator, am. In fact, I am about to find out, as I tell the story, who I am and why I am telling it.

There's only one thing I know: the title: *The Loneliest Man on Earth*. This title came to me some time ago, and I thought it would be a good one to use. I thought it might be a little embarrassing if my family and friends (those who I still considered to be friends, that is) should see it—to admit that I, the potential author of this story, should be, or even pretend to be, the loneliest man on earth. That is, at the present time.

Others could have claimed the distinction years or centuries ago, I am sure; but I am the only one who is currently entitled to the honor. I am the loneliest man alive today. There may be women who are lonelier, but certainly there is no man. And in case there is any doubt, I am a man and intend to stay one.

I'm beginning to figure out, or shall I say—discover—who I am. Now I know. I am a person who was originally named Harold Ubring—but I always hated my name, so I changed it to Hugh Bring. That's my name now: Hugh, like a color, a hue. It feels colorful to me, and that's why I continue to use it.

I realize, of course, as I tell this story, that the truth is beginning to come out. In other words, the truth about my life is appearing in my mind. Therefore I am recounting it in a form that can be understood—for it's best to be understood by a majority of people.

It's true: I went to a seminar once and the speaker said it's dangerous to be too unique. Better not be too unique. Can you believe that? He said if you were too unique, they wouldn't know what to do with you.

Well, that's how I feel. I'm too unique and no one knows what to do with me. That's why I'm the loneliest man on earth. No one knows where to put me. No one knows which shelf I belong on. Is my life a fiction? Is it a biography? Am I gay—or lesbian—or is my life an action/adventure? How could I possibly know? I'm a total enigma to myself; and therefore to the rest of the world.

But let me get to the story. It's coming back to me now—it's about these lessons I used to give. It began with Alice, the bartender. At exactly 11 PM every night, even though it was against the law in New York City, she lit up. Everyone would cheer and light up along with her. Even I did. When it turned 11, it was time to light up.

And what a thrill it was, breaking the law. Laws are meant to be broken after all; and since the only meaningful law is to live by your *own* law, I never saw the harm in lighting up and defying the mayor and governor. At 11 PM, everyone was happy again, just like in London. Smoking and drinking together, as they were meant to be enjoyed; not one at a time (smoking outside and drinking inside) but together.

On this particular night, however, something seemed wrong. Something seemed out of place, as if the alarm were about to go off. Alice said, "Oh no, what's going on here? Hugh, honey, what's happening there?"

"What do you mean, Alice?" I asked, as if smoke were fumigating out of my ears or something.

"Hugh, you've got smoke coming out of your ears!" she cried.

"What?"

"You do, honey. I swear. What's going on with you?"

"I don't know. Anger, maybe? Angst, I guess. I'm anxious about my life. I'm anxious about living, about surviving in this city, I guess."

"Honey, come here," she said. "You've got smoke coming out of your ears and I better fix it."

Then Alice did something that was truly kind. She pulled me off to the side of the bar and started performing an X-rated activity on me—right there in the corner of the bar! It had been a long time since a woman had done anything like that to me (I usually preferred men to do that sort of thing) yet it was a thrill to have this experience so unexpectedly; and apparently it worked, for she told me soon after that the smoke had stopped coming out of my ears.

I thanked her incessantly, gave her a big tip, and left the bar, heading back to my home.

I felt as if I were being followed the whole time—strange, I don't know why, but I had the distinct feeling that someone was following me home. I turned, I looked—but no one was there. Yet I still sensed that someone was following me.

I arrived at my apartment on Ludlow Street. I unlocked the front door and walked up three flights of stairs. I got to my door and I turned—and there he was—he had followed me all the way home— there he was: the man of my dreams had followed me home and up my stairs, unbeknownst to me.

"Who are you?" I asked.

"Why, I'm the man of your dreams. Get real, Hugh. I'm here for the lesson."

"Lesson?"

"That's right, the lesson you promised me."

"Oh yeah, come on in."

I opened my door and invited him inside. His name was Stud. Really, that was his name. Everyone knew him by that name. Everyone *I* knew, at least, which was hardly anyone. But he swore that his name was Stud and we all believed him.

We were a bunch of foolish idiots in those days. We believed anything we could possibly believe to make ourselves feel better. Ah, to feel better about ourselves. If it improved our self-image, we believed it. As sure as the afternoon followed the morning, as sure as the morning followed the night.

To believe in something comforting is a good way to start the day, like waking up and believing in strawberries. Knowing there will be strawberries in your cereal, that's a great faith to have in one's day. It helps the waking process. Or anything similar. Knowing there will metaphorically be strawberries in your cereal of life will help you get through most anything, even the idea that there's nothing awaiting you in the approaching day, nothing that will greet you with affection, with tenderness.

Most people don't know this. Most people aren't that unique. They know what shelves they belong on. They know who they are, what jobs they have, what parties they will go to and which spouses will be the ones intended for them.

But you see, I never knew any of these things, so as I led Stud in for his lesson, I realized that I wasn't at all prepared for it. I said, "Hey, Stud, what lesson would you like me to teach you tonight?"

He responded with his usual courteousness, "Whatever lesson you think would be most appropriate to teach me, Hugh."

I thought for a minute and then said, "OK, Stud, I will teach you the lesson of how to behave in this world."

"That sounds like some lesson," he said.

"Oh yes, it's a lesson that keeps on teaching. For once you know how to behave in this world, you will always know what shelf you belong on. And once you know what shelf you belong on, you will never have to be lonely again. And if you are never lonely again—"

"But I'm not lonely," he said.

"I know, but I am," I confessed.

"Well, whose fault is that? Not mine."

"It's the fault of the shelves," I said. "There aren't enough shelves to go around. If we all have to fit on a shelf, then there aren't enough shelves to go around. It's as simple as that. We will have to be shelfless, without a trace of shelf-pity."

This happened about six months before. I don't remember anything more about that lesson or how I got through it. All I know is that I never saw Stud again.

I miss him now as I think of him. I miss the pentagram tattoo on his right shoulder; I miss the two-day growth of his beard, the faint smell of whiskey on his breath—and the way he shook my hand, smiling vaguely at me, as if to say, "Hugh, let me give you my strength. Everything is going to be all right, man."

And yet, the funny thing was—I was the one who was supposed to be giving the lesson. I was the one who supposedly had the answers. I was the teacher, the psychologist, the psychic.

But Stud vanished into the night, as did the others...and I never saw any of them again. That is, until I returned to the bar where Alice worked. I hadn't seen her for six months.

"Hugh!" she cried, "You look younger! What did you do to yourself?"

"What do you mean? I've been taking my vitamins. I've been to the beach. I exercise every day and I try to stay in shape."

"You must age backwards. You're looking good."

"So are you, Alice. It's good to see you."

"Have you been avoiding me?" she asked. "I haven't seen you since the night I stopped the smoke from coming out of your ears. But look— look who's sitting over there...."

I turned and saw a young man with bright blue eyes staring into space, smoking a cigarette, looking as if he were searching for an answer. I said, "Excuse me, Alice, let me say hello to this man. He looks familiar to me."

I went over to the table by the wall where the young man sat. I said, "Hi. My name is Hugh."

"I know," said the young man. "Don't you remember me?"

"Well, you look familiar—but no—I don't remember you exactly. Where do I know you from—was it here?"

"No.... You gave me one of your lessons. Don't you remember?"

"Not really. What did I teach you?"

"You taught me not to trust anyone. You taught me never to trust a single person except one."

"Except one?"

"That's right."

"Who was that?"

"Me," he said. "You taught me to trust myself."

"And have you proved to be trustworthy?"

"Yes and no," he said, his blue eyes glistening through the cigarette smoke. "I can trust myself up to a point. But then I start looking for

59

someone else to trust, and that's where I get fucked-up—and I can't trust myself anymore."

"Sounds like you get confused with who you are and who else is out there. You've got to stay with yourself. Never leave it—cause it's all you've got."

"Thanks, man. Will you give me another lesson?"

"Sure," I said, "but I can't do it here. We'll have to go back to my place."

"Where do you live?"

"Just across the street."

"Well, let's go then."

And I left the bar with Larry—that was his name. We went out into the night. We climbed my three flights. We entered my apartment. And I proceeded to give him the best lesson I had ever given. It was a lesson about life. It was a lesson about smoke. It was a lesson about the meaning of the universe.

But I remember nothing more about this lesson, for it was so long ago.

All I remember is Larry's bright blue eyes, searching for answers as he looked up to me with such hope, yearning for some meaning through the smoke that filled my apartment that night.

Six months later, I gave another lesson. My lessons seemed to be getting better and better; and I needed six months between each one so I could learn more about life. Every six months or so, I was ready.

I met Paulo, a Brazilian young man, in Tompkins Square Park one night. He was reading Paul Tillich's *The Courage to Be*. I walked right up to him and said, "Excuse me...I read that book in college—and I remember the last line after all these years."

"What's the last line?" he asked.

He turned to the last page to check my recitation, which was about God reappearing in one's life; and when I finished I said, "Right?"

"Exactly right," he said.

And we really seemed to hit it off. I gave him my story, *The Loneliest Man on Earth*, what I'd written so far, because he asked to read it; and he chuckled in places and made a few suggestions. He thought that everyone was unique, though; or that everyone *thought* they were unique. He couldn't pronounce the word very well, especially when he tried to say "uniqueness."

But I begged to differ with him. I told him that yes, everyone starts out being unique, it's true—but that most people conform—and lose—their uniqueness. I told him it's very uncomfortable not to have a shelf to fit on.

And that was the lesson in a nutshell.

I wasn't sure that he agreed with it; he was still very young, and perhaps still believed that he was unique. Though I was sure my lesson made an impression on him; I was sure that when he got older, he would realize that it's a choice. And oh, I knew this choice. I knew it with my blood.

I knew that Paulo would never forget my lesson, but I never saw him again. He vanished into the night.

I didn't give another lesson for six months…and when I did, it was to be my last lesson.

In high school, a Jungian analyst read my Tarot cards. I'll never forget this experience. He told me that I was different from everyone else and that I wouldn't find happiness until I accepted the fact that I was different—and accepted it as my strength. It has taken me many years to come to terms with this; and now, as I look back on my last lesson, I can see that it all makes sense, that life is rich with rewards if we follow our inmost heart. Sometimes it takes many years, though, to find what is there.

My Last Lesson:

It was a rainy night in September, just after Labor Day. My name was Hugh Bring and I had a story to tell. I took my story out of my apartment with my umbrella. I walked down three flights of stairs and onto the street. Ludlow Street, New York City, the Lower East Side. Cool neighborhood. Everyone smoked and rode bicycles.

I went into my favorite bar and saw my favorite bartender, Alice. I loved her. She was the only woman in my life.

"Hi Alice, I brought you my latest story."

"Oh, Hugh, I can't wait to read it! What's it called?"

"I'm not sure. I was going to call it *The Loneliest Man on Earth*, but now I'm thinking of calling it *My Last Lesson*. Which one do you like better?"

"Hmmmm…that's a tough call…not exactly my department. I think I like the first one."

"Well, here it is…it's almost finished. I'm in the last section right now."

"I'll try to read it tonight. Thanks, honey. Want a drink?"

"Better not. It's going to be a late night. Just came here to get dry and give you the story. Gotta go now...."

"Bye, Hugh, see you soon...I'll let you know what I think."

"I know you will...bye!"

"Don't get too wet!"

And of course, I never saw Alice again. At least, that's what I thought at the time. I never went back there. I never returned to Ludlow Street or even my apartment. Or so I thought. I went out into the rain, but it had stopped raining. As soon as I popped my umbrella open, it stopped raining. But then I couldn't keep the umbrella closed. Every time I closed it, it popped open again.

Finally I said, "Fuck this," and threw it away.

I kept walking.

I walked over to the East River. I walked along the FDR Drive. The clouds disappeared and the moon rose in the east, like it always does. It was a waning moon. It was late. The FDR Drive was quiet. No one was around.

Suddenly I felt a shiver, a slight wave of fear. I turned around and there was a tall man standing next to me. He was a handsome man with whiskers. I lost any fear I had and said, "Hi there."

He said in a deep voice, "What are you doing, walking out here on the FDR Drive all by yourself?" He sounded pretty stern and I thought I was getting a little scared again.

"Are you a cop?" I asked.

"No, do I look like one?"

"Yes, as a matter of fact, you do—but don't worry, I'm into cops."

"What do you mean by that?"

"Oh, just kidding. I'm Hugh." I offered my hand to shake, but he didn't take it. He looked at me strangely, his eyebrows askew. He was very serious. He didn't break eye contact with me. There was an intense mixture of suppressed fear and sexual stimulation; and I wondered what kind of scene was about to transpire, there on the FDR drive, without a car or person in sight, with the clear sky and the waning moon shining on the two of us.

He took out a small pistol and smiled for the first time, pointing the pistol right at my chest.

I honestly didn't feel afraid. I felt very calm. I said, "You can shoot me if you like, but first, will you let me give you one of my lessons?"

"You gotta be shittin me," he said, laughing, still pointing the gun at my chest.

"No, I'm serious. I give lessons. I'd be glad to give you one before you shoot me."

"Well, jeez, now I've heard everything. And just what kind of fucking lesson do you think you're gonna teach me, huh? That it's bad to kill people? Bad to take their money? Bad to blast their fucking brains out cause I've got nothing better to do?"

"Actually, you get to choose your lesson. I'll teach you anything you want."

"And what makes you the big authority, asshole? What makes you equipped to teach lessons? You got a PhD or something?"

"No PhD, that's one of the reasons I can do it so well. I don't have too much education. How about you? How far did you get?"

"High school. I graduated high school. Plus one year of college, but I dropped out. What the fuck—why'm I talking to you?"

"You're talking to me to learn something." My voice got a little bold here: "Now what kind of lesson do you want? I don't have all night."

"All right. Teach me how I can find some peace of mind. If you can do that, I won't kill you. But you better talk fast—no tricks, understand?"

"No problem, but could you please stop pointing that gun at me?

64

It's hard to think when you're doing that, you know?"

He put the gun in his pocket and started cracking up. "This has got to be one helluva night to write home about. All right. Shoot—I mean, let's get started."

"We've got to go back to my place. I only give lessons at home."

"You have got to be shittin me, asshole. You think I got no brains?" He took his gun out again.

"No, I think you're very intelligent...and very good-looking, too. I'd like to have you over, offer you a drink, and give you your lesson. I promise I won't try anything tricky; and if you're not satisfied at the end of the lesson, then you can shoot me and I won't interfere. I promise."

"You are a whacked-out dude, I swear. What'd you say your name was?"

"Hugh."

"Shut up."

"What do you mean?"

"That's my name, too."

"What!?"

"That's what I said, name's Hugh."

"Really. This is interesting. Hugh's not my real name; it's what I go by." A taxi was slowly approaching. "Put the gun away. Let's get into this cab."

Hugh and I drove north on the FDR Drive. We had to turn around at 23rd Street to head back south to Houston Street...and hang a left on Ludlow.

We passed my favorite bar and stopped at my building. We got out and climbed the three flights. I opened the door, we entered, and I locked it behind us.

Then Hugh pushed me up against the wall. He had one hand

around my neck and the other on my shoulder. It felt like he was going to strangle me. His beautiful eyes were glazed over with a spirit so intense that I could only be turned on in response.

I gasped for air: "What's going on? What're you doing?"

"Nothin," he said, right up to my face. "I just wanted to scare you. I'm not really a violent guy—if you believe *that*! I just wanted to test you," he laughed, letting me go.

"Oh yeah? Well, maybe I'm testing *you*." (I was starting to get brave.)

"Maybe it's a mutual test...yeah, right? What've you got to drink?"

"Jack Daniels and peach schnapps."

"Together?"

"No, stupid. Separately. You don't strike me as a peach schnapps guy. You want some Jack?"

"Sure." He took out his pistol again.

"You can just put that away till after the lesson's over. Here. Give it over. Give it to me." I held out my hand.

"You have got to be kidding, A-hole. Just get me the drink."

"All right. But no shooting till after the lesson."

(I realize that this may sound a little far-fetched; but I assure you, I am recounting this evening, this evening of my last lesson, as accurately as I remember it happening all those years ago.)

We sat on my couch and drank. He sat right where Larry sat, and Stud before him, and many others. We lit up. We smoked. We stared at each other. And finally I said, "So what kind of lesson do you want?"

"Peace. I told you. I want peace."

"All right. But you'll have to trust me on this one. Can you do that?"

"I don't trust anyone."

"Well, just trust me a little, OK? If you want peace, you've got to trust me for a few minutes, OK?"

He didn't answer.

"Give me the gun. I'll give it back to you. I swear."

"And what if I don't?"

"Then you lose."

Much to my surprise, he handed me the pistol right away.

I stood up and aimed it at him. I cocked it. I made believe I was going to pull the trigger—not that I was an expert on how these guns worked exactly, but I pretended I knew what I was doing. I tried to look convincing.

But he didn't do anything. He looked like he was waiting for me to kill him. He took a drink. He took a drag. Finally he said, "Please...."

"Please what?"

"Please...do it...." And he started to break down. I couldn't believe that this strong, handsome guy was crying in my apartment.

I kept pointing the gun at him, but finally I said, "I can't do that. I promised I'd give it back to you." And I did.

I sat down.

He gave me such a look of disbelief, such a disappointed look of dismay, as if he simultaneously lost and found his faith in human nature. He slowly recovered, took out his handkerchief, blew his nose and put the gun in his pocket. He said, "Was that the lesson?"

"Yeah."

He finished his drink and put out his cigarette. He got up and started walking to the door. He unlocked it, opened it...paused for a moment, and gave me a salute. And then he left my apartment with the door open. He vanished into the night.

I never saw this man again, but I knew it was my last lesson. Because I realized something, and it was good, I guess, to realize it. After all the lessons I had given, after all the learning I had achieved in between the lessons, while anticipating the next ones, I realized that I had fooled myself. I had deceived myself. I had convinced myself of something that I weirdly thought was right.

But I knew that night that I had been wrong: I was not, nor had I ever been, the loneliest man on earth. In a way, in a very strange way, I realized that I was the happiest man on earth. Well, maybe not the happiest exactly, but perhaps, one of the most sane. Because in my own insane way, I had found what it meant to be myself; and in so doing, I didn't need to give any more lessons. I didn't need to learn what I was teaching anymore.

I finished my drink, put out my cigarette, and went out into the night.

I thought I'd say hi to Alice before closing time to see if she read my story yet.

JEWISH AMERICAN PRINCE

1

Screw the people who say I shouldn't tell my story in the first person. If I'm going to tell this story, what other person could I possibly tell it in? Third? They say that if you speak about yourself in the third person, it means you're schizophrenic. And if there's one thing I'm not, it's schizophrenic. Oh no, not me.

I know because I asked my former shrink once. He said I definitely wasn't schizophrenic. He said if I were schizophrenic, I'd know it. Or—I think what he meant—is that others would know it, not me. He also said I wasn't manic-depressive or obsessive-compulsive. I was disappointed. I thought I was at least obsessive-compulsive. But he said no, I wasn't any of these. Just plain neurotic. I think this guy was dim-witted. That's why I stopped seeing him.

I'm actually my own version of all three: a little schizophrenic, a little manic, more than a little depressive, and I'm sorry, definitely obsessive-compulsive. How else do you think I'd have the determination to tell my story? Do you know what it takes to do that? A whole lot of neurotic obsession, I'll tell you.

So let me begin. I'm not going to begin at the beginning. How boring. Let me skip the first twenty years. You'll miss a lot of sex with girls and guys, but why don't we start with the juicy stuff. Let's skip to age 26. Let's skip to my brainwashing, to my joining a cult. That's a good place to start. Since it was the turning point of my life, it's a good place to start. Most people don't know their own minds anyway. So it's good to *think* you know your mind, lose your mind, and find a new mind after. At least that's what happened to me.

So let me begin.

I was sleeping with this woman who went there. She was my scene partner in acting class. At the last minute, our teacher switched partners on us and Kat and I were thrust together. The teacher must have known we'd be a good match. Or maybe she wanted to save me from my queerness, who knows? But it was a brilliant choice on the teacher's part; and screwing Kat led to many things in my life, one of which was the cult she was trying.

I liked it more than she did (the cult, I mean, not the sex). She said they all walked and talked like robots. But I thought they had some interesting things to say. I got hooked. And Kat left. She broke up with me. No more sex, just friends. I stayed at the cult, Katless. I got very brainwashed. I thought it was the greatest knowledge the world had ever known.

I almost had a nervous breakdown. I got a prescription to Valium because I thought I was going to go crazy. The psychiatrist who gave me the prescription really scared me. I was having these panic attacks, you see, because I didn't know my own mind. He asked me (before prescribing the Valium, which was the only reason I was there) if I ever thought they sent me special messages on the radio.

I said, "You're scaring me! Why are you asking questions like that?"

He said, "They're just routine questions to determine your state of mind."

"Well, you're freaking me out and I wish you'd stop," I replied. Then I added, "Well, whenever they play Wagner on the radio, I think that God is doing it just for me, but other than that, no, I don't think they're sending me special messages."

He said that was fine and gave me my prescription.

I was afraid to take too much; I didn't want to get hooked. I only took it if I thought the floor was about to give out from under me—and sometimes I thought that; sometimes it got really scary. I was so afraid of having a nervous breakdown—how would I explain it to anyone? I'd be so humiliated.

So I tried very hard and never had the nervous breakdown. Though secretly I think I did have it, only I didn't have to go to the hospital. I just stayed home and went crazy. I didn't know it then, but it was the best thing that ever happened to me. After a year at that cult, after being brainwashed and unbrainwashed, I was set on the path to know who I was, which took another 26 years, but that's another story. That's for another book. I couldn't stand to write more than that. I don't have that much patience, though I try.

Being Jewish really makes you neurotic. It's built into the religion. It's built into the family. Freud knew it. I used to love to walk into cathedrals and breathe the incense. Jews never had incense. We had Torah. Hey, I don't mean to offend, but it's true: all Jewish guilt comes from the Torah. Tell it to my mother. We're born that way. It's as natural as matzah balls. You eat the matzah balls, you die of Jewish guilt. But first you spend years at the shrink, trying to figure it all out. You may go to a cult, get brainwashed. But you can't escape the Jewish guilt. It eats you alive.

It took me years, but I *did* escaped the Jewish guilt, though I'm getting ahead of my story. Let's get back to the cult. Every person has to examine his or her mind sooner or later (unless you want to be mindless) and getting brainwashed in a cult is one of the best ways to do it—*if* you can escape. I still see some of those robots walking around. They're still living their cult existence—they're still there. But if you can go through it and escape, it's one of the best lessons you can ever learn, better than anything you can read in a book: You learn something, you believe it, and then you unlearn it. That's necessary with all education, true, but with a cult it happens at super-speed. You can learn a lot about yourself if you're strong enough.

And I've always been strong. I've always been an individual. That's my problem in the world.

So let's go back to the days of the Cult, the naïve days of New York in the Seventies when I was young and getting to know myself. The world seemed young also, getting to know itself too. Truth was something I craved, something I searched for, and something for a while I thought I'd found. On the corner of Mercer and Spring, I thought I found it. The greatest knowledge the world had ever known. And I was going to be their spokesman for humanity.

2

I signed my name in the *New York Times*, saying that I "changed from H." That's what they called homosexuality, just H. As if the word was really bad to say in its entirety. I was one of a small group who signed their names in *The Times* for the Cult. We thought the greatest knowledge the world had ever known should be advertised. I think we had to pay to be in it, it was such a privilege. But I'm not sure about that now; I don't remember exactly.

Proud as I was to sign my name, though, and proclaim this knowledge to the world, the worst thing—the thing that started the panic attacks—is that after I signed my name, I started getting H attacks. They told us at the Cult that it was perfectly normal, just like an alcoholic desiring a drink. BUT...I had said I'd changed—permanently—from H, so how could I be like an alcoholic? The H attacks got worse...which led to the panic attacks...which led to the shrink and the Valium.

We had a running joke at the Cult—the group of guys I was with who said they'd changed and signed their names along with me—we had a joke we used to chuckle about strictly amongst ourselves: We used to say, "I've changed from H with the exception of Arnie Feldman." Arnie Feldman was this gorgeous stud of a guy and all of us who had changed from H were still attracted to him.

Funny (as an aside), years later, I see him walking around the Village with his wife Mary, whom I'd had one date with. She told me I wasn't manly enough, that she liked football player types. Well, she got Arnie Feldman and they walk around the Village together, now two middle-aged people probably still believing that the Cult is the greatest knowledge the world has ever known. I've always been dying to stop them and tell Arnie the joke we used to tell about him; and though I've got a lot of balls usually, I don't think he'd appreciate it. He really was quite a stud. Changed from H with the exception of Arnie Feldman. Hah!

You know, I don't believe in sin, never have, even with my Jewish guilt, but I have committed one and only one sin in my life: I was using my student card from the Cult to buy me a student locker at the Saint Marks Baths. Isn't that terrible? There I was, changing from H, and I got a student locker at the hottest H place in town. This was before they closed the bathhouses. This was the Seventies...Donna Summer's "Love to Love You Baby," was the background music. I committed a grave sin, but Jews don't have confession, we only have ourselves to torture—endlessly. There was and is no actual sin, of course, but the reason it was a "sin" was because of my hypocrisy. I wanted to have my cock and eat it too—at the student rate.

Kat never knew about my trips to the baths. She said I was a really good lover, better than most of the straight men she had ever been with. I loved to hear her moan, "Oh, Jim, Oh Jim, it feels so good, it feels so good. Ohhhhhhhhhhhhh." I prided myself on my prowess with women. I even convinced myself how turned on I was. But, you know, secretly, I think I was turned on by my own manliness making love to a woman. Maybe not. There were times I felt truly turned on to her.

But toward the end of our relationship, I remember seeing her standing naked in Vermont, looking beautiful after a shower. She was all lovely and everything, but she was missing something—and it freaked me out to realize it—she was missing a cock.

So Kat turned out to be the last woman I slept with. I enjoyed them all. It's fun to experiment, especially in one's pot-smoking days, but it's also good to find out what you like:

H.

H I was...and H I'll be...forever.

H and proud.

3

Now don't get me wrong. I wasn't unhappy being H. I may have been unhappy, but it wasn't because I was H. Every H guy there was miserable being H; I was the only one who wasn't. They called me the Happy Homo. I was there for other reasons. I was there to understand life.

Little did I realize at that young and tender age, that life cannot be understood in a rational, linear way. The Cult had it all spelled out for you. If you followed their line of questioning, you would eventually be a happy person in the world.

There was a certain force that these people had, walking down the aisle like Nazis; they really seemed to know what they were talking about. I used to get very nauseous at their seminars. I thought I was going to throw up, and since I always had a great fear of throwing up—a phobia, in fact—it was not easy to take all that knowledge into me.

One day I ran out onto the street, terribly nauseous. I ran smack dab into Matthew from college. It was embarrassing. He chuckled, "What's the matter, Jim, the Cult getting to be a little too much for you?"

The only reply I could think of was, "Yes, I guess it is."

I wish I knew at the time that nausea was a great sign of danger. Something deep in the pit of my stomach told me to stay away. But they had me brainwashed into thinking that a part of me WANTED to reject the greatest knowledge the world had every known, so I didn't trust myself. Kat had had the right idea.

Something in me, though, was drawn to the strictness of the Cult. Everyone was very strict and formal. You addressed everybody by Mr. or Miss—no Ms. Somehow I wanted a form for my life and I was convinced that I'd found it, despite my nausea. I was determined to stay.

I had thirty sessions (where the real brainwashing occurred) with three men sitting across a table from me. They fired questions at me. The sessions were taped and we were supposed to listen to them. The question I remember most after all these years was: "Mr. Friedman, what do you believe in most—magic or logic?"

Of course, the "correct" answer was logic; and I had believed in magic, as if magic was a foolish thing to believe in. Well, you know what? Years later, I believe in magic all over again; I have realized the fallacy of believing in logic, as if the world were organized in a logical way. But these people weren't mystics. They believed everything could be explained, just like the Freudians. Dangerous people, these logicians. They lose all sense of mystery.

4

The day the advertisement came out in *The Times*, I did a foolish thing. I made copies and sent them out to everyone I knew, including my parents' friends. I wanted to tell everyone about the greatest knowledge the world had ever known. People thought I was crazy. I suppose people have always thought I was crazy, at every stage of my life. But this was surely one of the craziest things I had ever done. And I never even minded being H until that damn cult convinced me that I minded it.

Two things helped me enormously when I was having my private nervous breakdown. One was the books of Rajneesh, AKA Baghwan, later called Osho. Page 11 talked about the fallacy of borrowed knowledge and I burst into tears as I read it. It saved me from the tangled web of my mind.

The other thing that saved me was a new psychic friend. I had wanted to see the original psychic from the Ansonia Hotel who predicted a group of "pseudo-sophisticates" a while before, which I had forgotten about. But he was out-of-town so I fell in with his cohort psychic, a man named Charles, and he took care of me then. He told me I wasn't having a break-*down* but a break-*through*. And he was right. I think he really wanted to get me into bed but he never succeeded. Guys in their twenties just don't realize how cute they can be—and what cockteasers they are.

That was definitely me. I was an actor then. I was singing on the subway one day and started smiling at an older man just because I was in such a good mood. I remember I was wearing my red, white, and blue T-shirt with a big star on it. I flirted with him and he invited me into his office uptown. He turned out to be a big agent. But I just couldn't go through with it. He tried to kiss me on his couch and I said, "Is this the casting couch?"

He said, "No! I don't have a casting couch."

I said, "Well, it sure seems like a casting couch." I was so obnoxious in those days. An obnoxious, spoiled, Jewish American Prince, that's what I was. Had I given him a few kisses, maybe I'd have become the star I'd always dreamed of being, never would have joined the cult, never would have gone through the many fucked-up years I went through, never would have become brainwashed, unbrainwashed, and gone through all my many misadventures . No, prick that I was, I refused his advances, I maintained my integrity, and lost my biggest chance of being a famous actor. Perhaps I would have considered it had he not gargled with Listerine right before the Casting Couch. There was a sink there and I could smell the Listerine. Made me totally sick. I could never kiss him after that.

So I was thrown out of his office. Back to pounding the pavement. Back to being a struggling actor. I could have had it all. Fuck integrity.

Anyway, Charles took me under his wing, and every time I felt a panic attack I could either take a Valium or call Charles or both. Charles had a very soothing voice. He wasn't as good a psychic as the original guy, but he made a good friend until one day he dropped me. Left me high and dry. I think it was because I insulted him. He asked me how I liked his hair tonic. I hated it. I thought the smell was disgusting, like an old man's barber shop smell. Almost as disgusting as Listerine but not quite.

Why do people have to wear such nauseating scents? They turn a lot of people off, especially hot young boys. Now that I'm older, maybe the boys are turned off to *my* scents, don't know. I'll have to keep that in mind, be more careful of what I'm wearing. I stopped wearing Patchouli for that very reason. Turned off too many people, especially my Jewish family.

I wasn't allowed to put my jacket or backpack in my sister's bedroom. She said the whole place reeked of Patchouli after I was gone. I simply thought that anyone who didn't like Patchouli wasn't worth knowing. It's supposed to be a love and money attracter. I hope it didn't turn away the hot young boys!

Anyway, I lost all my friends at the Cult, lost my girlfriend Kat (even lost her as a friend because I tried to convince her she was making a big mistake by leaving the Cult), lost the psychic, lost the agent, lost all my old friends because they wouldn't come to the Cult, lost my new friends because I was crazy as a loon. I just had my Rajneesh books and my family. What a combination.

But I was about to lose them too. I was about to lose everything: my family, my apartment, everything. Little did I know that my greatest life adventure was about to begin. In the streets of New York, I would find my way...but before I found it, I'd have to be very lost indeed. For being lost can often be one of the best things in life.

ACKNOWLEDGEMENTS
(previously published in)

People of Shambhala + The Spiritual Survival:
Adventures on the Magical Path, Actor Turned Psychic, The Potential for Genius

Scroll of Thoth:
Adventures on the Magical Path (excerpt)

NEXT Magazine:
International Psychic, Wagner's Ring and The Wizard of Oz

Literary Vision Magazine:
The Concious Egoist

Ashé Journal:
The Loneliest Man on Earth

The Holy Male:
Jewish American Prince

The Wizard of Washington Square

Kyler James has been a professional psychic counselor for over 30 years. A Wiccan high priest of the Gardnerian tradition, he started reading Tarot cards on film sets as an actor, having studied with the great Stella Adler at NYU. He has published two novels with Rebel Satori Press: *The Secret of the Red Truck* and *Mercury's Choice*—and is happy to be publishing his first collection of fiction and nonfiction with Rebel Satori. Having read Tarot cards at many restaurants in New York, he is now well-known as "The Wizard of Washington Square," where he reads people from all over the world.

kylerjames.com

Author photo: Justin Aversano